For Elaina
You'll always be my
"Little Pip"

BLACK ROSE writing™

ISBN: 978-1-61296-740-0
PUBLISHED BY BLACK ROSE WRITING
www.blackrosewriting.com

Printed in the United States of America
Suggested retail price $13.95

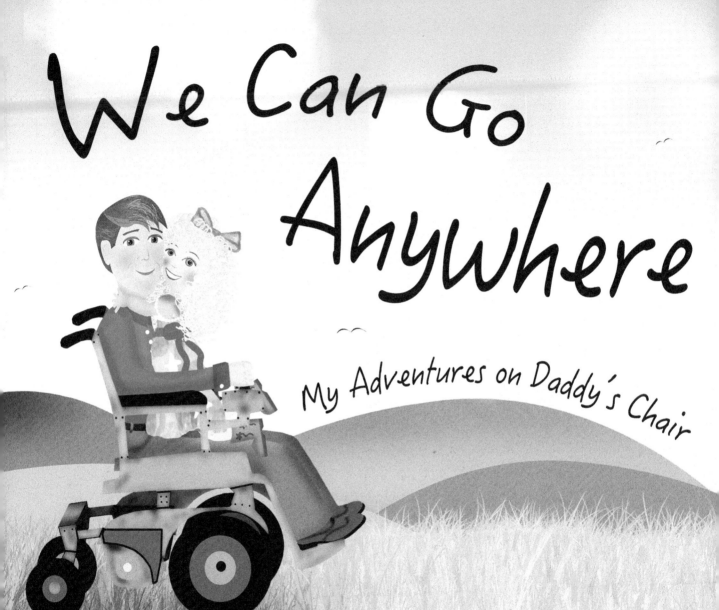

We Can Go Anywhere

Anywhere

My Adventures on Daddy's Chair

Written by Glen Dick   Illustrated by Linda McManus

Hi, I'm Elaina and I have curly hair.

This is my Daddy, he has a wheelchair.

I know it may look like just a wheelchair.
But when I'm on his lap, we can go anywhere.

Adventure awaits around every bend.
We can be anything if we just pretend.

Like a boat on the ocean,

or a plane with two wings.
My Daddy's wheelchair can be many things.

Our adventures take us far from home,

to places where wild animals roam.

Sometimes he's a stroller when we need to go far.

Sometimes I'm a driver and he's my race car.

He once was my walker when I couldn't walk myself.

Now he gives me a lift to reach a high shelf.

The rides at the mall only go up and down,
but Daddy and I can spin round and round.

Riding with Daddy doesn't cost any money,
I save my quarters and he tickles my tummy.

When my wagon is heavy and getting too full,

I hook it to Daddy and he gives me a pull.

He's a horse for a cowgirl, riding out west.

He's my comfy chair when I need a rest.

We pretend we're a fire truck off to the rescue.

Or a train on the tracks going Chugga choo choo.

Now he's a tractor plowing for my crop.

Today we're a school bus and we make every stop.

He's a carriage for a princess going to the ball.

But he'll always be my Daddy,
and that's my favorite one of all.

About the Author

Glen Dick never let his spinal cord injury in 1995 slow him down. He went on to work with children through Big Brothers and in an Elementary school. His adventurous spirit and creative nature allow him to push his limitations. Now with a daughter of his own he finds new adventures through her sense of imagination and wonder. This is his first children's book. He lives in Chalfont , Pa with his wife and daughter.

About the Illustrator

Linda McManus is a photographer/artist. She received her BFA from Arcadia University. Her career includes architectural photography for builders, architects, real estate brokers and others. Her fine art photographs have been shown in local exhibitions. Linda's nationally selling collection of commercial art has been licensed, applied to greeting cards, framed art and more. Linda graciously donates her talents to a variety of charities. She lives in Bucks County, PA with her husband, two boys and "canine daughter" Zoe.

CPSIA information can be obtained
at www.ICGtesting.com
Printed in the USA
BVOW05s1207060817
491151BV00017B/58/P

9 781612 967400